FORTY-TWO

A SHORT SCIENCE FICTION STORY

SUPER GREAT CHALLENGE STORIES
BOOK 8

RYAN M. WILLIAMS

Glittering Throng Press

PO BOX 179

RAINIER WA 98576-0179

eBook ISBN-13: 978-1-946440-92-1

Paperback ISBN-13: 978-1-946440-93-8

GTP NO. 50
SGC NO. 08

ACKNOWLEDGMENTS

This story is one of 52 weekly stories written (and published) over a year. It's part of the Super Great Challenge (SGC) run by Dean Wesley Smith and Kristine Kathryn Rusch through the WMG Publishing workshops on Teachable. Without that challenge, this story (and the others) likely wouldn't exist.

Additionally, in creating the cover art for the stories in the SGC, I've typically used Blender—my **favorite application ever**—an open source, free, 3D modeling, digital painting, animation, sculpting, and video editing application. I've taken courses and watched tutorials from creators like Ducky 3D, Southern-Shotty, Grant Abbitt, Curtis Holt, the Blender Studio, CG Cookie, CG Boost, the Blender Guru and so many others. It's a wonderful and inspiring community.

And I'm so grateful for the **support of my members** on my site (ryan mwilliams.com) for their encouragement for this challenge. My family has also been instrumental in making this possible. It helps immensely having people behind me on this journey. Thank you.

———

CHAPTER 1
FORTY-TWO MINUTES

The final interstellar object (ISO) detected by the Vera Rubin Observatory wasn't the first, or the tenth, or even the hundredth such object recorded in the Rubin sky survey. Over the last few years Rubin had revolutionized our understanding of interstellar objects—a frankly terrifying result. It was clear that we're basically on an interstellar firing range with fast interstellar objects shooting through the solar system from all directions. Fortunately for us, space is vaster than most people imagine—more vast than they can imagine, without being trained as an astronomer, astrophysicist, or cosmologist. We might be on the firing range, but we were a tiny speck in the solar system. The "bullets"—asteroids, comets, and other debris propelled by supernova explosions or expelled from other stars during formation—had an extremely low probability of actually hitting anything in the solar system. The only part of the solar system slightly likely to be impacted was Sol, our star, the Sun. Everything else in the solar system makes up a tiny percentage of the total mass of our local environment. There just isn't much that could get in the way of any interstellar objects shooting through the system.

But the chance wasn't zero. We only had to look at Uranus knocked over on its side or Venus with its retrograde motion to see evidence of those impacts. Possibly caused by other bodies during the formation of our solar system—but more likely impacts with objects from outside of the solar system to cause such extreme variations. Space is mostly empty of baryonic matter, but sometimes a connection still happens.

Looking at the screen with the highlighted result and the projected passage through the system, I ought to have slept with Mike when I had the chance. Too late now.

I was alone. In my apartment. The Rubin observatory was halfway around the world from me, but that didn't matter. I could do my research anywhere, so why Olympia (that's in Washington state)? Inertia. *My inertia.* I hadn't planned on living here, but its where I ended up for undergrad. I stayed and did my graduate studies remotely on-line. I got married. Divorced. Still stayed in Olympia. Moving seemed like so much trouble.

It was after 10 PM. Raining outside, pretty normal for September. My apartment is a two-bedroom. I decorated this one to use as my office and my YouTube studio. I work for the university, adjunct professor, and on the side I do popular science videos about space and astronomy. *Inspiring the next generation.* That's what my channel says. The ad revenue from my videos is a welcome addition to my limited salary. I got the bookshelves behind my desk for a great deal when a couple upstairs moved out because they bought a house. That wasn't in my future. It wasn't really an investment when the mortgage on a house would take me a couple lifetimes to pay off.

My gaze went back to the screen. I *really* should have fucked Mike.

I had one foot up on the desk. I'd been painting my nails a dark teal color and it wasn't dry yet. The nail polish odor stung my nose. The only lights in the room came from my curved monitor and the desk lap with the stars on the purple shade. Light-blocking black curtains covered the room's two windows. In the darkest corner, next to the bookcases, Lucifer stirred on the cat tower. Mostly visible only from his glowing eyes. From outside came the sound of a siren. For a second my heart leapt, thinking (*irrationally*) that it was because of what was on my screen. As the siren faded, I realized that didn't make sense.

No one knew what I knew. There were facts displayed that no one was *ever* going to know.

The one-hundred and forty-second interstellar object detected by Rubin was going to be the literal answer to the human race on the question of life, the universe, and everything. The only answer we were ever going to get, in…

forty-two minutes. I shit you not.

Fucking perverse sense of humor, the universe has.

All my emotions had their hands up, demanding attention, and I couldn't give them the time. I didn't have the time. Somehow, in the highly improbable events of the universe, Douglas

Adams had known. He probably didn't know what he knew.

I remembered the hitchhiker's motto. It didn't matter. There wasn't time for panic. Or even tears.

I was already down to forty minutes. *How had I looked at the calculations at precisely the right moment to get that initial estimate?*

If my parents were still alive, I could have called them. I'd love to talk to my mom, and my dad, again. They'd sit together and we'd FaceTime and it was almost like I was back in Idaho with them. Later, I'd been glad that I *wasn't* in Idaho with them, as the state made a run at being the farthest *north* of the Southern states.

Thirty-nine minutes. I looked at Lucifer's slitted eyes. "What are we going to do, Lucy?"

CHAPTER 2
THIRTY-EIGHT MINUTES

No parents to call. A dark apartment. Nothing much in the fridge for a last meal. I got up from my fancy ergonomic chair and stood up, feet bare against the vinyl flooring. I slipped my phone into my back pocket.

"Lucy? You hungry?"

"Meow." It came out as a high-pitched cheep. Eyes opened wide, glowing in the light from the monitor. I'd already fed Lucifer dinner earlier, but the glutton was always ready for a meal. She might as well enjoy it.

Her soft paws were soundless as she followed me down the short hallway, past the accordion doors that hid the washer and dryer, to the kitchen. I flipped on the lights. She twined around my legs, a deep rumbling purr vibrating through my calves and shins, alternating as she pressed against both.

I took down two cans from the cupboard above the counter. One was her standard cat food, an unappetizing brown mush that she loved, and the other was a can of tuna, saved for special occasions.

"One final feast, Lucy!" My voice sounded shrill to my ears. Lucifer didn't care.

I dished out the cans onto two plates. It was a lot of food for the cat who had already eaten tonight. She might be sick. But then again, she might not have time to be sick.

"Here you go." I placed both plates down on the kitchen floor.

Lucy went straight for the tuna.

Straightening, I ran a hand back through my short hair. The kitchen was clean. Not surprising, I didn't tend to make it messy. When I did fix something, I cleaned up afterward. From the floor came Lucy's happy smacking noises and purrs. She looked blissfully content. I bent, stroked a hand down her short dense fur. It was so soft. She arched slightly into my hand without stopping her feast.

"Love you, Lucy," I said. My throat tightened. I straightened.

I didn't want to look at my watch, but I did, of course. *Twenty-three minutes.*

My breath caught. I pressed a hand to my chest and felt my heart hammering.

CHAPTER 3
TWO WEEKS AGO.

The dating goddesses had smiled on the evening. Only a few clouds drifted across the night sky. The Moon was full. Between it and the glow from Olympia's lights, there weren't many stars to see overhead. That was fine. I wasn't looking at the stars, I was looking at Mike.

A science teacher. We'd met through Tinder (*surprising, I know*). I thought he looked like a young Paul Rudd (*or older, he doesn't age*), with the same sort of amused grin and twinkling eyes. I thought Mike was probably taller than Paul Rudd. He was certainly taller than me—most men are when you're only five foot three inches. He wore an actual sweater vest (*blue*) over a white but-toned shirt and fitted khaki pants. His shoes were the sort of hikers popular with people in Olympia. No glasses, which sort of surprised me, because *science teacher*, seemed like they went with the job.

He was standing in front of me, close, and was playing his fingers of one hand against mine. "I had a great time. I should have you come talk to my class, introduce them to an actual scientist. They'd love it."

I was already shaking my head. "I didn't go into my field to teach kids. Deliberate choice."

"You teach college students."

I laughed. "Barely. When I can keep them awake."

Was he going to kiss me? I wanted to kiss him, no question. But if I kissed him first, he might take it as an invitation for more and as much as I wanted to, I didn't feel like getting burned by the first seemingly nice guy that I'd met through the app.

"May I call you again?"

I nodded, grinning, thrilled he'd asked.

"Great." He leaned in, I looked up at him, and he gave me a quick peck on the cheek.

On the cheek. I think I stopped breathing. I wanted to grab him and pull him back, but I didn't. I restrained that impulse, and other impulses. He stepped back, hand going into his pocket.

"Okay, then. Have a terrific night." His car (*a nice, sensible Kia sedan, white*), beeped. Then he got in and drove away.

CHAPTER 4
TWENTY-ONE MINUTES

left Lucy enjoying her final feast and walked into the living room. I dropped onto my couch (*a forest green, velvety cat hair magnet*). I picked up one of the many pillows and hugged it. The TV on the opposite wall was a large dark square, dimly reflecting the room. The remote sat on the glass-topped wood coffee table I'd picked up at an antique store. It must have been from the Seventies, old, with thick, darkly-stained wood that had been carved into flowing shapes and flowers. I loved it.

I pulled out my phone. I had colleagues and friends I could call. Misery loves company, right? No one else knew about this, I was sure. I swiped to my feed and spent a few of my seconds scrolling for any news updates or alerts. *Nothing.*

Why would there be? The Rubin observatory produced so much data every night, observations could take forever to study and analyze. Plenty of other people were looking at what had been gathered, but it was unlikely that anyone else would have looked at that particular recent dataset. They probably would be studying older data. And if they weren't focused on ISOs, they'd be looking at entirely different things. So I could call them. I could sent out a bulk email. I could alert the media. Hell, I have my own YouTube channel, it'd make sense to post a video explaining what was happening. I'd get credit for a discovery that no one wanted.

For the next nineteen minutes.

Less. I'd have to go live. I didn't have time for anything else.

A knot of fear loosened a coil and moved, showing itself like the xenomorph in the shuttle at the end of *Alien*. (*If you haven't seen it, its too late now, and what's wrong with you? That movie is older than my coffee table.*) It wasn't fear of the ISO rearing its ugly head. It was a more dangerous fear. *What if I'm wrong?*

"Hellscape," I said to the quiet room. I *wanted* to be wrong, of course. But there was that part of me that asked what would happen if I went live, shared what I knew, and turned out to be wrong?

If I wasn't wrong, only a few people would ever see the video. If I was wrong, though, it could be the sort of thing that haunted me for the rest of my career. And it wasn't like there was a single fracking thing that could be done about it, right or wrong. We have zero-capability to handle this sort of situation even if we had years to prepare and instead we have—

CHAPTER 5
FIFTEEN MINUTES

I wasn't going to sit on the couch for the next fifteen minutes wallowing in my regrets and fears. *Yes*, I should have fucked Mike. It wouldn't have completed my life. *Yes*, I'm afraid of being wrong—but I've never let that stop me. Not from going to school, to pursuing science, research, and teaching. I've gone live with other ISO discoveries.

Which got me back here, back to my desk, explaining to all of you what Rubin detected, how the orbit was calculated, the math using the object's albedo and rotations to determine its size. It isn't a dinosaur-killer, you can see the difference on the screen. This is a planet-buster object. It's possible an impact like this turned Venus into what it is, busting apart the planet and the reforming with a reversed rotation. It's the sort of thing that could knock Uranus over on its side. The type of thing that formed the Moon in the early days of our solar system.

Five minutes.

I silence the alarm and look at the camera. I smile and blink to clear my eyes. "You might see it now, depending on where you are, as a bright spot in the sky. It's going to look like it is directly overhead for those of you in the Northern hemisphere, in North America. The angle of approach and the Earth's own rotation and movement are bringing us together.

"Mike, I'm sorry we didn't get more time."

CHAPTER 6
TWO MINUTES

My eyes remain dry now. I see the 142nd Rubin ISO through my window. It's the brightest thing in the sky. The light is casting shadows outside on Olympia's streets. It's reflected in the bay. People are going outside, looking up at the sky. For some, it might be the only time they've paid so much attention to what is in the sky above.

All of the astronomy boards, chats, and streams are blowing up now with everyone going live. I've got the latest data coming in and my computer is processing the numbers, constantly refining the estimate…

CHAPTER 7
FIVE MINUTES

t is decelerating. *Has* been decelerating. We hadn't seen it yet. The data we had was relatively old.

CHAPTER 8
FIFTEEN MINUTES

I went to the bathroom and got one of my blue towels. I've got it across my lap. Lucy is on it, stuffed to her whiskers. She's probably going to go into a coma with as much as she ate.

CHAPTER 9
FORTY-TWO MINUTES

Remember the words of our prophet—don't panic. It isn't what we—what I— thought, but it is an answer to so many questions. It's going to be crazy. I'm not going to be able to sleep, so I texted Mike and asked if he wants to come over.

I mean, the future is always uncertain, right?

———

ABOUT THE AUTHOR

Ryan M. Williams is a full-time career librarian and a multi-genre writer with over twenty books. He writes across a range of genres including science fiction, fantasy, paranormal, mystery, horror, and romance. He earned a Master of Arts degree in writing popular fiction from Seton Hill University and a Master of Library and Information Science from San Jose University. His short fiction has appeared in Pulphouse Fiction Magazine, On Spec Magazine, and anthologies from Pocket Books and WMG Publishing.

ALSO BY
RYAN M. WILLIAMS

POEVILLE

The POEVILLE series with feline detective
C. Auguste Dupin and his human librarian
Penny Copper might be just the thing.

•The Murders in the Reed Moore Library

•The Task of Auntie Dido

MOREAU SOCIETY

Brock Marsden, a genetically-modified
detective, solves the toughest cases in a this
far future space opera series.

•Dark Matters

•The Gingerbread House

•Past Lives

•Past Dark

DEAD THINGS

Do you like your fantasy dark and
paranormal? Ravyn Washington isn't like
other students. Her grandmother was called
a witch and if the Inquisition discovers
Ravyn's abilities she could burn in the
DEAD THINGS series.

•Waking Dead Things

•Dreaming Dead Things

•Killing Dead Things

FILMING DEAD THINGS

Filming the Inquisition at work made Stefan Roland's ground-breaking documentary directing career—calling him the Jane Goodall of Dead Things.

•Farm of the Dead Things

•Mall of the Dead Things

•War of the Dead Things

•Trailer Park of the Dead Things

SCIENCE FICTION STORIES & NOVELS

Discover more science fiction with these books.

•Infestation

•Europan Holiday

•Stowaway to Eternity

•Crunch Bang: The Chrystal Eagle Stories

•Space Monkeys: A Short Science Fiction First Contact Story

•Invasion of the Book Snatchers: A Short Science Fiction Story of Small-Town Terror

ROMANCE BY KATE N. RYAN

And if you like romance and comedy, the books by KATE N. RYAN will tickle your funny bone—and more.

- Watching You Sleep: a laugh out loud romantic comedy

- Tom Scratch: A Short Fantastic Romance Story